FEELINGS IN A WHISPER

"Seasons of Eternity"

By

Grafton Pressley

(Janet's 1st Cousin)
(Fannie Graves sister - Jim Bell Pressley's son)
Grafton was a well-known Methodist Pastor

© 2004 by Grafton Pressley. All rights reserved.

No part of this book may be reproduced, stored in a retrieval system, or transmitted by any means, electronic, mechanical, photocopying, recording, or otherwise, without written permission from the author.

First published by AuthorHouse 04/29/04

ISBN: 1-4184-5880-5 (e-book)
ISBN: 1-4184-4883-4 (Paperback)
ISBN: 1-4184-4884-2 (Dust Jacket)

Library of Congress Control Number: 2003099948

This book is printed on acid-free paper.

Printed in the United States of America
Bloomington, IN

Table of Contents

Friends 2
Season With You 3
Daffodils Dance 5
Spring in the Heart 6
A Power Over Me 7
Alone With You 8
Back with You 9
Brief Touch 11
Diamond Tears 12
Dream of Me 13
Echo of My Heart 14
Eloquent Words 15
Feel the Quiet 16
Feeling You Here 17
Friends Forever 18
Friends Together 19
Getting Free 20
Go Down Quietly 21
Grass, My Confidant 22
How Great It Is 23
I Did Not Know You 25
I See a Tear 26
I Wonder If You Know 27
If You Will 28
In A Night 29
January's Chill 30
Kindness 31
Language of Denial 32

My Secret	34
Naiveté is a Friend	35
One Touch	36
Quietness	37
Season of Reaching	38
Shared Dream	39
Shared Life	40
So Close	41
Songbird	43
Special Love	44
Sunset Ritual	45
Tear Path	47
The Child Within	48
The Memory of You	50
The Mirror I Need	51
Old World	52
The Time Came	53
Time Slipped Away	55
To Touch	56
Today	57
Two are Gone	58
Whisper of the Pine	60
Wondering If You Knew	62
Words on Soft Lips	64
You are Enough	65
You Are Everywhere	66
You Looked at Me	67
You Smiled a Yes	68
Your Tears Ran Down	70
Who is this "YOU"?	71
My Christmas Carol	72
To Carol	72

Ours Alone*	73
Autumn	76
Season of Letting Go	77
A Flower's Kiss	78
A Fresh and Holy Wind	79
Awakened	80
Being Real	81
Calvary	82
Christmas Baby	83
Creation's Womb	84
Dan	86
Susan	88
Ease Me	89
Eternity Moves	90
Finding the Path	91
Fragrance	92
Freedom to Love	93
Gift of Life	94
God Answered	95
God Praying	96
In A Whisper	96
God's Gift	97
God's Reach	98
God's Tears	99
Holy Star	100
Image of God	102
In A Tear	104
Into the River	105
Jesus, Quiet and Still	107
Joy Vibrates	108
Just Wondering	109
Leaving Worries	111

Life is a Tiny Seed	111
Life Slipped Away	112
Lord, Give Me Wings	113
My Gratitude	114
"One Breath Poems" III	115
No one is Older or Younger	116
No Room in the Inn	117
Old Crosses	119
One Day	120
One Sin	121
Running Deep	122
Prayer for Peace	123
Quiet River	124
She Found Strength	125
Shepherd's Heart	126
Still, Deep River	127
Sweet Chariots are Coming	128
One-Breath Poems IV	129
The Pauper's Prayer	130
Share the Warm	132
The Song of True Rest	133
Thirst No More	134
Tomorrow I'll Create a Man	135
What is Going to Be	136
Where You Are	138
You Are Mine	139
Young as Thirty Three	141
Your Creator	142

Feelings of Spring

Part I

"One-Breath Poems"

Spring is the feeling of love unfolding...
releasing a fragrance like flowers
along the path to the heart.

Memories of you,
like photos from the fifties,
have a tinge of gold and
the value of diamonds.

Friends

In these pages
you will meet
lifelong
and eternal friends.

You will not know
who they are
by name
and place.

But I will,
for they have
given poetry
to my life
and
to my forever.

Season With You

There is a feeling
in the touch
of a light wind moving
that takes me back
in time
when the aroma was new.

Not Spring.

It gives a companion feel
beside me and in me, warm.

Not Summer.

It has the low sound
of laughter and an unending smile.

Not Fall.

It has a warm feel, a fire
that sends its message deep
in the heart.

Grafton Pressley

Not Winter.

Wherever and whenever this breeze
touches me
I am free
to see who is there.

My heart knows
it is you.

It is the season that never ends.

Daffodils Dance

Daffodils dance
on white snow flakes.
Spring is born.

Life is awakened
that has never existed
until God gave birth
to a new season.

Spring.

Spring in the Heart

Spring awakens
the heart from its sleep.

The soul stirs
and catches
forgotten feelings
that rise again
to the top.

The mind is caught up
by the buds giving birth
to new colors never seen.

The birds
come home singing
love rituals
and making nests
for their babies.

God moves his hand
across the land
and everything
is new.

All life applauds
for an encore.

A Power Over Me

I can spot her
in the distance
among hundreds
on the beach.

Like a compass needle
I am drawn to her.
I feel her walk.

I love her manner
and the imprint
she has left
on my mind
and heart
for the rest of
forever.

She has a power
over me
that I love.

Alone With You

When I stop
and feel the treasure
of my life,
you come to heart.

The feelings I shared
with you
come back,
washing the clutter
of little things away,
such as years
and space.

I see you standing there
young as you were
when I was but a breath away.
And, I am new again.

Better still,
is knowing that
even the power of time
is not enough
to steal what I shared
alone with you.

Back with You

In a dream I returned to
college days.
My feelings led me there
in pursuit of what
I may have left behind or missed.

People appeared
that I have not seen
for forty years or more.
They seemed to know
why I was there
and offered plans
to help me find or bring back
the very thing my dream
           had dared to recover.
I searched the campus and
           my old room.

I even ventured to the attic
and found a potted plant still intact.
There was a prized old radio,
papers done but never turned in,
seeds were there that had never been sown.
I would bring them back, I thought,
to water and see them grow,
catch their scent

Grafton Pressley

and experience the beauty
of something never finished
many years ago.
I found more than I could take.

But the thing
I prized most,
I never found.

What I miss is you.

Brief Touch

Our feelings
touched so briefly,
and so deeply,
then continued on
as a spring that never dries.

They are refreshed
with each memory
that turns me back
to you.

Diamond Tears

The tears I shed
the *days* we parted
are diamonds now.

Under the black pitch
of walking away,
and looking back
until you were gone,
they hardened bright.

Like a million years would do.

But for a broken heart,
it doesn't take that long.

They are priceless,
as are the memories
of you.

Dream of Me

Remember me
in your dream tonight.

Any role will do
as long as it is loving
and awakens you
in the morning
with a glad smile
because
I touched you
last night.

Echo of My Heart

There is an echo
in my heart...
calling you.

I feel it now
as a clear spring,
bubbling without end.

I hear it
repeating your name
in quiet drumbeats.

It rides
each sunset,
kneeling in silent ovation.

The performance
never ends.

Eloquent Words

You worked hard
at knowing what to say
lest your words
embarrass us both.

But a glimpse
of the light
behind your eyes
spoke more eloquently
than words
what you wanted
me to feel.

The beauty of the thought
almost took my breath.

It was the very thought
I had of *you.*

Feel the Quiet

Feel the quiet
struggling within
our words.

Trust it.

Lean in to it.

Feel it.

It is what we hunger
to experience
together,
alone.

Feeling You Here

A warm telescope
in front of me
could bring you
much closer
from your west coast
hide-a-way.

Better still,
would be
for you to appear
in the magnifying glass
of my eye.

Best of all
would be
to feel your touch
and catch your breath
with my pounding
heart

Friends Forever

Once friends,
you and I,
we can
feel the warmth
of its power
forever
as though it is
today, everyday.

I feel it now
thinking of you.
I am returned
to the beginning
when we discovered
that mystical power
as a tide rising
within us
while being together.

You and I.

Friends Together

When I look back
over the years,
I always see you.

I am both glad
and sad.

Glad, because
we shared our lives
for a season.

Sad, because
we could not be friends
together through all the
seasons of life.

The nearness I crave
is more than memories.

It is the taste
of your being here,
under the tree,
to share the fruit
of what we began
when we were
friends together.

Getting Free

I meet pain
and turn to avoid it.

I turn further
and the pain pursues.

I am addicted to running
and thus, avoid
the confrontation
that will set me free.

Go Down Quietly

Go down quietly

into the clover's

crimson bloom.

Catch the aroma,

feel its fingers

walking slowly,

gently,

to the word

you want to say

while looking back

at me

with a smile

more eloquent

than the word.

Grass, My Confidant

I see grass as my friend,
trim
and fresh,
flexible and bending.

I see her as a friend
to sit with,
to stroke
and to touch.

I know her as a bed
where I can lie down
with a friend,
to whisper, caress,
and know
she holds everything
in confidence.

How Great It Is

Many times our good-byes
were short lived.
Like, you were gone
with the night.
And then,
we were one again.

Between our good-byes
love grew
and drew us closer still.

Our last good-bye
ended...
the way it was.

But I am thankful
that it could not end
memories
that pop up
like the sunrise
and color
a path across my heart.

Our last good bye
was the beginning
of distance

Grafton Pressley

and the march of time.
But not an end
to how great it was,
and is,
each time I think of you.

I Did Not Know You

I held your hand
in the night
and did not know you
until morning's light.

What I felt,
and then
what I saw
will never leave me.

I am glad.

You encourage me to be
what I can be
and what I want to be
for you.

I See a Tear

As I look
into your smiling eyes,
I see a tear
rising and sliding
down your cheek.

There is a prism
of colors
speaking quietly
the words
you want me to hear.

"It is a tear
of love
as you look
at me."

I Wonder If You Know

I wonder if you know
how many days of my life
I have thought of you?

And how many times
my heart has skipped
with the feeling of you?

I wonder,
would you be glad
or sad?

Glad is my feeling.

And each time it happens,
I pause to pay homage
to an eternal friend
who is distant in time,
yet as close
as a heart beat
and as refreshing
as each morning's
new creation.

If You Will

If you will
look warmly
through my eyes
into my heart,
say,
an hour or so,
you will see things
that are kind to you.

And whenever
you are lonely or alone
and need a gentle friend,
I will be there
in the mental image
you carry of me,
burned into the feelings
of your heart.

Then you can rest with me
until the anxiety is gone.

In A Night

In a night of loneliness
I picked a star
and gave it your name.

There is no other like it...
or you.

You are the fingerprint of God.

Watch the other stars pass by.
One day you will hear your name.

For I call it with my thoughts
that ride the light rays
from creation's eye
in the heart of God

reaching infinitely near
to find a warmth
where we are alone
together.

January's Chill

January's chill
covers us with
heavy coats
while the fire
burns inside
our zippered prison.

We struggle
to escape
with desires intact
and find warmth
in a naked world
already burning
its way through
the maze of layers
pulling us to
the place
we hide
from one another's view
until we are there.

Then, in the warmth,
we know it is right
to be here linked
where our hearts
promise comfort
in January's chill.

Kindness

You can never
do a kindness
too soon
because
you will never
know
how soon
it will be
too late.

Language of Denial

He talked incessantly.
His 5-year-old son
had drown in a pool, resuscitated
and put on a vent.
The doctors did not use the term
"brain dead",
but that is what it meant.

The dad talked on…on.
The estranged wife
refused to go into the room
while her husband was there.
"It is **his** fault", she kept saying
from her secluded place on another floor.

The dad talked on, "He is my best friend, my buddy.
He will be all right. He and I play pitch. He could be
a professional baseball player one day."

All that kept him alive was the vent
and the entanglement of his separated parents.

After exhaustion, the dad left for a break.

The mother came in.
She wrapped her legs around his lifeless body

and said she would **never** leave his side.

"He has not been to school yet.

He will start in the fall."

The doctors wanted a family gathering

to discuss the option.

It never happened.

His body shut down

alone,

on its own.

My Secret

As deep as I go into the past
I can remember my secret.
It is in one of the hands
behind my back.

Which hand
is part of the secret?

If I open it for you
will you still love me?

If you take its gift
you'll know me
and love me more.

My secret
is waiting there
for you and me
together.

Naiveté is a Friend

She has whispered
"courage"
in my ear
when I would have
run away
in fear
and failure.

She has
given me
sweet successes.

I love her
for that
and
she loves me.

We will
spend our lives
together,
happily
as one.

Naiveté.

One Touch

One touch
can dissolve
an angry standoff.

One touch
can shatter walls
that hold back
reservoirs
of love.

It is the touch
of honesty and confession
at the beginning
of a new start.

Quietness

Some things sound better
when unsaid,
like, "I promise,"
when I don't.

Or, "I love you,"
when it is cheap.

And, "I am sorry,"
when I am glad.

Silence is eloquent
when it is true.

Quietness is music
waiting for a song.

Season of Reaching

If you are reaching out
feeling for a name
of someone calling you,
reach again
for I am here
reaching out for you.

Eventually we will touch
and know the search completed
that has pounded in our hearts
throughout a lifetime
and into heaven
where we'll know
no bounds,
and reach
      becomes touch.

And voices
seasoned by time,
love and waiting,
will meet
and become one.

Shared Dream

The dream I had
was too beautiful
to have dreamed alone.
You took my hand
in a meadow
mid the fragrance of
a million flowers
with colors
I have never seen.
You sat leaning against a tree
by a cool, fresh spring
that bubbled melodies as a harp.
You invited me to sit beside you
as you placed my hand
in your lap.
You caressed my cheek
and whispered words
too valuable
for a mind to conceive
or a memory to hold.
You awakened
a part of me
that has never lived
until you held me
in our dream
last night!

Shared Life

I am glad
to have been
a part of your life.

My hope is that
I am still.

But, if not,
I will understand.

And I will live with the comfort
that in the life to be,
you will be a part of my life again...
with the freedoms
that only eternity can give.

So Close

Sometimes I grieve
knowing that we came so close
to living life through...
together.

The timing was so close.
Maybe in our hearts
it was right all along.
Maybe we waited to be certain.
And after the waiting was over,
when we were ready to commit,
time had passed us by
and we stood miles apart
wishing we were ...
together.

Miles, hours, and years do not take away
what I felt for you.
And still,
in a way that is safe
for those to whom
we have given our lives,
the feelings will always be there,
as real as the eternal image of you
I carry in my heart...
together

Grafton Pressley

All we had to give
we gave to another.
All they had to give
was given to us.
And it is adequate...
together.

What can I say,
or dare say,
except,
I loved you and always will,
both close and at a distance...
together.

Songbird

The songbird
awakened me today.

In a frenzied rush
I dashed into the day.

Suddenly,
remembering
something left behind,
I turned.

In that moment
of turning,
the songbird whistled Its song.

I stopped still, and
I listened,
listened,
listened to the wisdom
in the melody
of that songbird,
sent by God,
for people
such as I.

Special Love

I stumbled into your life
as an anxious child,
afraid and timid.

You held my hand
and dared to tell me
that I was special
               to you.

You have changed me
               forever.

I will always love you for that.
I have been loved
by the best.

Sunset Ritual

Come kneel beside me.
Going down together
we will make the sun
bend more quickly to touch
the mirror still lake
with its likeness.

Go down slow with me.

The sun's image is rising up...
up, to touch its maker.
He will move down now,
slowly, into the image.
The two will become one.
"See it. There it is...
a perfect circle."

Now a blanket of orange
is being spread.
It is the invitation to let go.

Watch now as the image
fully accepts the sun.
Are you comfortable down here?
I am ... with you.

Grafton Pressley

Maybe we could stay here
and read the stars together.
I expect we would like what they say.

The morning sun will awake us...
if we let it.

Tear Path

The tear clinging
to your blue eye
speaks volumes.

The tear path
that streams
down and kisses
your smile
tells me
what I want to hear...

You love me this much!

The Child Within

I see the child within her
as she stands by the bed
of her dying husband.
She weeps as she speaks
hoping he will *hear*
and
praying that he will *answer.*

"I'll love you to the moon and back,
a million times and more."

She rubs his forehead
gently, as a child
rubs the fur
of a dying kitten.

The pain is felt
two times and more.
The little girl within
and the wife
by his side.

Will he live again?
Yes!

Both will feel
the touch
of the living God,
a million times and more.

*Written for a Decatur friend, Juanita Dillard,
after the death of her husband.*

The Memory of You

I see you in the faces
of others
who are near.

A twinkle in the eye,
a feature in the face,
or a smile
can change in a moment
to a memory of you.

It is so good to see you
as often as I do.
My heart leaps
to where you are
and back again.

I will never tire of leaping
and would run
if I knew I could see you—
even for a little while.

The Mirror I Need

Holding a mirror
in front of me
I see myself
as one with you.

We walked in the
rising and the setting sun
seeing things
we laughed about
and named them in a way that
we alone would know.

Things like berry bugs,
and
tracing our faces
in the Milky Way
and laughing
at how we looked
together.

We cried
as a wave of sadness
rained our dream away,

but never from the mirror
we carry in our heart.

Old World

Old world,
you've been a faithful home.

You are the playground
of my childhood,
an arena to my passing years.

I have walked your fields.
I have touched cool springs
with parched and thankful lips.
I have been energized
by the cool breath
of a sudden summer rain.

I have looked into your
infinite star filled sky

My mind has
been stretched with awe.

My heart stays young
knowing you have loved me
through the hands and hearts
of those I have touched
on this short journey home.

The Time Came

The time came
and took you far away.

We thought the light
would burn forever
and its glow
would bring us together again—
like forever burning—
pulling like two moths
being moved to their flame
kindled out of a desire
such as we knew.

Gradually,
sadly, the light lost power.
I know the sadness.

The embers of memory
remind me with its
continuing embrace
of pleasant thoughts
that drew us together
many years ago.

Grafton Pressley

I wonder what you are doing today,
and with whom you share
your loving light – forever.

Someone who deserves the best,
I pray, for "you are special".

I still feel your fingerprints
caressing my heart.

Time Slipped Away

Life slipped away
on silent
chipmunk feet...

Present
for a little while,
then burrowed
forever in
eternity.

To Touch

To touch
and to be touched by you,
even for a moment,
is a magic rush
that has changed
the chemistry of me —
forever.

Every thought
of that mysterious touch
brings it rushing back again
like a tide,
like here and now
in this moment.

You have awakened my soul
from its somber sleep.

Today

Tomorrow
is somewhere
I have never been.

So, I live today
as though
it is my last.

I can always
look back
and
dream.

Today, I live.

Two are Gone

She looked forlorn
lying on the sod covered grave
of her just buried husband.
The only thing feeling good
were the sod squares still green
and the flowers made cool
by the evening air.

She said sadly,
"It is not worth living without him."

The family could not lift her or her spirit.
The cemetery man said he had to close.
Two men in white coats came.
They asked if they could help in some way.
She declined by saying,
"I'll just be here awhile longer."
They hoped it would be soon.
Her car was there.
The motor was running.

She never went anywhere.
They found her next morning
with a pistol by her side
and a bullet in her head.
She stayed there

until she could "be with her husband".
The motor was *still running*.
The birds were singing
like they serenaded her to sleep.
The flowers were fresh, fragrant
and glistened with the dew
of the morning that awakened...
with two of her children
gone.

Whisper of the Pine

Walking here,
stopping,
holding a tree
as a comforter,
I hear them sing
in a melodic song of love.

Pines know me,
for I am one with
the earth as they.

They speak
with the taste of bark
that hides their lips,
but I feel their kiss
as mine.

We are one in our quest to live...
now and forever.

They are older than I.
Their seed
was scattered
and grown
before God
would make
one like me.

FEELINGS IN A WHISPER

He knows there are days
when I will stop to find solace
in the soft embrace
and the whisper of the pine.

Wondering If You Knew

My eyes followed you
through the room
wondering if you
knew that I was there.

And if you did know,
would you turn my way
and look for me
or even smile.

I heard you ask
if any one had seen me.

Your face lit up
with a smile
when you heard
that I was there
in the same room
with you.

My heart bounced
in my chest
as we crossed
the room,
not seeing any one else.

FEELINGS IN A WHISPER

In those few steps
I was already hoping
that our meeting
would begin a chapter,
maybe a book
or whole library.

But at that moment,
as we crossed the room,
I was thankful
for that very first
word we would speak.

Words on Soft Lips

You breathed warm words
from soft lips.
A feeling I did not want to lose
passed into emotion
and was permanently
fixed there
for a lifetime of pleasure.

The next words
had a parting sadness
that said goodbye
underneath your tears
and mine,
and the soft rain,

Words on soft lips
are not forgotten.
Decades are speaking,
even now...
and I am sad and glad.

You are Enough

I have not seen
the Eiffel Tower
or
the Great Wall
of China.

I have seen you.

I hold
your willing
and eternal spirit...

that is enough.

You Are Everywhere

You are in the beauty
of each sunrise of joyful color.

You are in the smile
of every friendly face I see.

You are beside me
on every path that I take.

You are under the cover
of a lonely moon each night.

You are with me
in my nearest dreams.

You are with me
to awaken in the morning.

I awaken with you.
But you,
you are not there.

You are everywhere.

You Looked at Me

When you looked at me,
my heart stopped
it seemed.

My eyes turned
shyly away
then quickly
back to you
in hope that
there might be a smile
we could share.

It happened
in a flash,
a brief second
at most,
but it was enough
to tell me
that what I saw
awakened the beginning
of a lifetime
I wanted to share
with you.

You Smiled a Yes

When you smiled at me
and said yes,
I felt
that we could
be happy together,
forever,
anywhere.

We can do with what we have.
The grass for a bed
and a peach tree,
our dining room with it's limbs
as table and chairs.

A menu is there.
It says, "Peaches in season
and fresh water from above
with choice of rain or dew".

The warmth comes from the sun
and the cool is in the night.
Our comforter
is being together,
touching.

Our entertainment center
is there...
in how near is it down to the ground
and how far is it to the nearest star.
Our clock is the moon
that rocks us to sleep
in its quarter cradle.

Good night, my dear,
I'll see you in heaven
in the morning.

Your Tears Ran Down

Your tears ran down
and mingled with mine
as cheeks touched
and hearts ached
with the pain
of separation
we feared
would be forever.

I am thankful
that forever, never ends.

There will be
many reunions,
if only
in the heart.

We will be one again
in time or beyond,
where love
is life and breath,
and we are one
in God.

Who is this "YOU"?

The **"you"** in these poems
can be one or many persons.

You have the freedom to choose,
or to guess.

It can be, really, **"you"**...
if you like that.

Or, if I claim complete safety,
the **"you"** is **my muse.**

She is always unreachable
and always near.

My Christmas Carol

I walked the earth
in darkness
looking for a light
to brighten and warm my way.

Then I met you
during Christmas of '58.

Since then the light
has grown brighter and warmer.
The light is my love
for you.

To Carol

Who has been with me
as these poems
were first conceived
in the womb of a heart,
who became
a midwife to assist
in the delivery
to the minds and hearts
of those who read
and hear these
"Feelings In A Whisper"

Ours Alone*

There are so many things
that are ours alone.
No one else can touch them.
Our first time to hold hands,
you squeezed mine
and my heart is still dancing.

Our first kiss,
our first Christmas together
say "who you love".
a sweater of blue.

Our trip to Kentucky together for our wedding.
Our honeymoon, wrestling, steaks, you and me.

Our first Sunday in our first church.
Our dog, Prince, Greg and Phillip.
We didn't know we could do that.

The special places are ours.
The woods where I grew up...
Lakeland. Sanibel. St. Simons.

There are so many things you have made
eternally mine. Like your laugh, tears,
my favorite soloists, beaches, smooth stones and seashells.

Grafton Pressley

Like sunsets, yard grass, golf grass,
hamsters, toy trains and bicycles.
Like cutting Christmas trees, ice storms and snow.
Like little league, Easter babies, mountain trips
and warmth when the bed is cold.
Like hope in a hospital room.
Like nearness when I am afraid of distance…
Like New York, the Holy Land and heaven.

I knew life with you would be great.
I just did not know it could be this great!

Do I love you?
Only until they make a better word!

* *from* **"Quietly Free"** *published in 1992 by Brentwood Christian Press*

Feelings of Autumn

Part II

"One-Breath Poems"

Life is a butterfly wing.
It must get you home.

Life is a dream,
to awaken is to know God

Bending low, I met God...
tall, caring, tender
and empowering.

Autumn

The season is

mellowing now

into colors

of every sunset

it has known

since creation.

Autumn

Season of Letting Go

When autumn leaves fall
I am reminded
of the many times
I have lost the strength
to hold on.

And in letting go,
as leaves do,
find new life
in the spring.

And I am restored
by the very God
who made the trees.

A Flower's Kiss

Like the butterfly's flight
with unexpected
flits and turns,
lifting, dropping.
never missing
a flower's kiss
or its sweet nectar,
so God has made us
to glean from each pain,
the nectar
of his presence.

"Is your life full of difficulties and temptations?
Then be happy, for when the way is rough,
your patience has a chance to grow." James 1: 2

A Fresh and Holy Wind

A fresh wind is blowing.
He is the Holy Spirit of God.
He is blowing away cobwebs
left on the soul
by neglect and self-centeredness.

He is blowing in fresh air
to replace that stagnated
by failure to change.

He is blowing in joy
to lift fainting hearts
left heavy by habit and form.

He is blowing in a new spirit
embodied in His people
moving into service
and love
as a wind moves
a sail.

Awakened

The sun
rose stealthily
to peak through
bedroom blinds.

One by one
it moved upward
to catch my eye.
I was awakened
to join you, God,
in celebrating
another day.

So many times
your Son
has brought
the light I need
to resurrect the soul.

Being Real

I can wear
a mask
that says I'm strong.

Or, I can be real
and vulnerable
to your weakness
and mine
and be healed.

Calvary

In silence
you can
hear
His
tear drops
still...

Like raindrops
on a drum
called Calvary's hill.

Christmas Baby

I picked up the aroma
of lightly smoking cinders
from the fire
warming shepherd's hands.

I caught a tune
of angel voices
singing of God's baby Son.

I was struck
by the radiant beam
of a star
that guided wise men
from afar.

God whispered
His message of love.

All the worlds in time
can hear Him still today.

A Christmas Baby
crying for His
family to come home.

Creation's Womb

Out of creation's
womb
new days are born.

Childlike,
free,
filled with colorful
choices.
Each day is a gift
of God.

It is a gift too great
to spoil or tarnish.
Most certainly it is
too valuable to lose
by filling it with
improper attitude
or revenge.

Like stars,
our days fill the panorama
of who we are.

Any day
is a miracle birth
from the womb of God
and holds within it
the power to rise or fall.

It is a choice.

Dan

I saw my soul today.

It was reflected like
a mirror in a friend
who sat across the table
and shared a feeling
that runs through him
like a deep current
that could move icebergs
in the opposite direction
of storm winds.

It is a core that runs
through me
at unpredictable times,
like a breeze through
wind chimes in my heart.

As he aged
he began to see
the dots of truth
connect into a beautiful
image of God.

He was flooded with insights
and discovery
that moved him to tears
and he asked,
*"Why couldn't I put it together
before now?
He is too beautiful to escape
or to describe."*

Susan

Like the aroma
of a flowering vine
she grew among us
leaving a fragrance
wherever she touched.

Her roots
grew deep in the soil
of our lives
as she searched deep
for a strength
that comes only from God.

Ease Me

Ease my panting heart, Lord.
I have run from task to task,
until
like a fire
they have parched the cells
of my spirit
and I thirst for
a *still island*
surrounded by you—
The Water of Life.

"He is like a tree planted by streams of water,
which yields its fruit in season
and whose leaf does not whither." Psalm 1:3 (NIV)

Eternity Moves

Time is a dimension
of eternity,
as significant as
an unheard sound—
yet, as real
as a baby's cry
drifting in on an east wind
as a sunrise,
and stirring history
with the birth of
God's Son.
Eternity moves.
It never leaves.
It is always present
as reality.

*"In the beginning God created the heavens
and the earth." Genesis 1:1 (NIV)*

Finding the Path

Lord,
I have lost the path
you gave me!
I am tired and blind
from exploring caves
and dead-end tunnels.

Pick me up
with your Light.

Like a good shepherd
holds a wounded lamb,
touch my wound with
your healing balm.

Help me to see
and to follow
your guiding light.

Help me to know your peace.
Help me to feel the joy
of walking your path
that leads to you.

*"Even if I walk through a very dark valley,
I will not be afraid, because you are with me."*
Psalm 23: 4 (NCV)

Fragrance

The fragrance
of the rose
is real,

like the presence
and the power
of God
who is with us
wherever
we go.

We are
never
alone.

Freedom to Love

If I understand heaven,
it is freedom
beyond the limitation
of a body.

It is life free of rivalry,
judgement and jealousy.
It is to love as God loves.
It is to love and to be loved
without limit.

We will sit at the
great banquet feast,
with people we didn't appreciate
in this life,
and discover
how loveable they are.

We will be joyfully united
with people we loved dearly,
but geography and commitment
restrained us.

I'll be there with you,
and you with me.
Freed by love.

Gift of Life

Birth
is no more
an accident
than the first day
      of creation.

It is the gift of life
and His never ending love.

It is filled
with all the beauty and glory
that I will allow.

God Answered

God answered a prayer today.
It was a little prayer
I prayed quickly.

The answer came
the next day.

"Oh, it was
just a coincidence"
some say.
"It would have happened
anyway."

I don't know,
maybe it would.
But maybe it wouldn't.
I just know
I feel better.
I feel thankful, too.
I pray on.

God Praying

I paused to pray
and in the quietness
I was surprised
to hear you,
God,
praying for me.

In A Whisper

The greatest truth
is whispered.

"I love you."

God said it

through His Son.

God's Gift

I come to you,
God,
asking for no-thing,
but knowing that
your generosity
cannot resist an
      opportunity
      to give
more than I would
dare to ask.

Your gift is always
greater than my desire.

God's Reach

God has no beginning
and no end.

He reaches in to
the depth of infinity
and touches creation.

He penetrates
distance,
time,
and sound.

He reaches into
the heart,
the soul and
the mind
of His people

and makes them
His throne.

God's Tears

Love drips
like a tear pouring,
POURING
from a broken heart.

It streams
through
a Savior's smile
to give birth
to every hungry
and fertile heart.

"As a deer longs for flowing streams,
so my soul longs for you, O God."
Psalm 42: 1 (NRSV)

Holy Star

Holy star,
we worship
your gift of light.

Our wisdom,
drawn to you
as a flower to the sun,
sought truth
and found that truth alive
and seeking us.

We heard His truth
through a baby's cry,
seaside stories of love,
the haunting sound
of nail torn flesh,
the whisper of forgiveness
and the shout
of mourners at sunrise
proclaiming the essence
of truth ...
He lives,
nothing can defeat us now.
We are eternally His.

Lord Jesus,
we worship you.
Lord, our Light of Life,
we worship you.

My Savior,
I worship you.

Amen.

Image of God

I saw myself
in the face
of my mother.
The distance
from here
to the mailbox
revealed it.
I had never
recognized it before.

It was like
looking into
an antique mirror
shaped by time
into the face
I see in every mirror
of my day.

Today, like never before
the image took life.
It is the face
of the one who gave me birth.
Now, for the first time
I know what it is

to be created

in the **image of God.**

*This poem was written in November of 2001. It was inspired
while I watched mother go to the mailbox to get her mail.
April 2002 she broke her femur. She died May 2002.
Seven months after this incident and inspiration.*

In A Tear

In a tear, still fresh,
Glows a rainbow
of promise
for all God's children
lost in pain and sorrow,
born from the hand of evil
gouging away the heart
of a nation.

That tear feels for love
in the ruin of Manhattan's soul
and the colors shine
as God's children rally as one
to lift the earth again
as creation
many millenniums ago.

Written after September 11, 2001

Into the River

Into the River
I move
with the current
pulling into
an eternal sea
of God's love.

Life happens
along the way.

A bird drinks.
A dragonfly hovers.
A reservoir is filled
and emptied.

The banks turn
and dart
while waterfalls laugh
or scream
down declining
rock walls
into ancient arms.

Grafton Pressley

The current
moves on
like a mother's love
to infinity.

      Into the river
I plunge
to catch God's hand
and trust his wisdom
over this slight gasp
called time.

Jesus, Quiet and Still

Jesus,
quiet and still
in his Mount of Olives
sanctuary,
sees hills
pointing to God
with eyes of light
glowing from oil lamps
in open windows
of Jerusalem's
hallowed space.

Bethlehem's light
calls him to remember
who he is,
his birth
as God's Son,
who is never alone
but the constant companion
to all he has given life.

Joy Vibrates

Joy vibrates
music in the heart.
Joy dances
as drum sticks
for the Great Drummer.
Joy sings
like the strings
of a violin
in the hands of its master.
Joy echoes
in the chambers
of the heart
making music
in all the events of life.
God's brush
turns darkness to life
and valleys into fertile fields
of the eternal harvest.
He turns fear
to mountain peaks of love
against the blue canvas
of the eternal sky.

Just Wondering

Sometimes
I wonder where I belong
and how I got here, where I am.
Some have more houses
than they can occupy.
Others have cars made for show or toy
and pay more taxes
than most folks earn.

Sometimes
I wonder where I belong
and how I got here, where I am.
There are the poor
who have one dress
picked from someone's
thrown out clothes.

They understand the *"poor of poor"*
who are needier still than they,
and stop to help someone
go through garbage or trash
to find a left over bite to share.
For they know how hunger feels.

Grafton Pressley

Sometimes
I wonder where I belong
and how I got here, where I am.

Just wondering.

Leaving Worries

I have discovered
that I can
leave worries
heavier than
footprints
on the beach,
and God,
stronger
than the tide,
will wipe
them clean,
forever.

Life is a Tiny Seed

Life is a tiny seed
buried in time.

It will not be
fully appreciated
until
it blossoms
in eternity
and reveals
the likeness
of God.

Life Slipped Away

Life slipped away
on silent
chipmunk feet.

Present
for a little while,
then burrowed
forever in
eternity.

Lord, Give Me Wings

Lord, give me wings
to fly above
the hurt and pain
I have allowed
to penetrate
my flesh
and heart.

Lift me
with truth currents
into the realm
of your perspective
and compassion.

Let me
fly free
in the eternal air
of your peace.

Lord, give me wings.

My Gratitude

The essence
of my gratitude to God is this.
When He looks at me,
his forgiven child, what He sees
is not my sins or accomplishments,
little or great they both may be.

What He sees is His own child
redeemed by grace
and adopted into His holy
eternal family.

"So if anyone is in Christ, there is a new creation: everything old has passed away; everything has become new!" II Corinthians 5: 17 (NRSV)

"As far as the east from the west, so far has he removed our transgressions from us." Psalm 103: 12 (NIV)

"One Breath Poems" III

Our Infinite God
Our Infinite God has no beginning or ending.
He has both. They are the same.

Life is a Dream
Life is a dream. To awaken is to know God.

A New Day
The night of the soul is a light on the path to a new day.

No one is Older or Younger

In the eternal calendar
of time,
no one is either
older or younger
than I.

We are children
of the same moment,
a puff of the
human dimension
and the same
breath
and heartbeat
of God,
our creator,
and home.

No Room in the Inn

"No room in the inn" is not a story line.
It is a hard reality when turned away
moments before a baby is born.
The long ride on a donkey's back
ended in a strange
and public street in Bethlehem.
Mary held her stomach
and Joseph's arm.
The time for finding
a bed had passed.
The baby was pushing.
Labor pains took control.

"Joseph, this is not a public thing.
Find something
or else you have this baby.

There is a stable over there in the dark.
It will have to do.
I'll go behind the animals.
If I'm noisy, they'll think it's the sheep.
Get ready to cut the cord.
***You** are a midwife, Joseph.*

Grafton Pressley

The swaddling wrap
is on the donkey's back
in the bag with the food and water.
Bring the water too.
This is ugly.
This is it."

It is cold reality.
But the baby came
and God provided.
Young shepherds came
to cheer and weep over the arrival
of God's own son.

The angels still sing today.

Old Crosses

Saws did not cut clean
back then
when Jesus
was nailed to a cross.

There were splinters,
sharp and aimed
at tender spots...
like
under a finger nail
or worse
under a broken heart.

They were dull nails
that took hammers to set.
Thorns gnawed
into the bony skull
of Mary's baby son.
Such love brought
my broken heart
to its knees.

One Day

One day at a time,
life slips by.
      One day
eternity
will open.
We will know life
as God knows it...
one act of love.

One Sin

I sinned
once.

It was during
a weak season

called life.

Running Deep

Lord, sometimes I feel slow
like the very edge of the river
that is soaked up by the bank.

Then I feel like the rapids
being hurled into the mist
of busyness and foam.

I want to be in the current,
running deep,
moving and being moved
by your power,
into the depth
of your ocean of love.

"If we confess our sins,
he is faithful and just and will forgive our sins,
and purify us from all unrighteousness." I John 1: 9 (NIV)

Prayer for Peace

Anxiously
I prayed for peace.
It was an urgent prayer
for God's intervention.

I was shown
an eternal well
with rustling,
bubbling waters.

I heard a voice saying
"This is the heart of God.
Wait quietly,
until the water is still
and you see your image."

Then I heard a whisper
from the depth within.

It was God,
quietly saying,
"Your peace is here."

Quiet River

Lord,
how long does it take
to renew a soul?

I've given the last morsel
of strength for so long
the reservoir is dry.
It has shrunk and parched
in the heat of expectation.

I confess, the giving side
has been wide open.
People reached in
and took what I didn't have.

I want to close the door
for awhile,
and restore my ability to
give from the overflow
of a still
quiet river.

Amen

She Found Strength

Her heart sank
like a well
on the day
her husband
suddenly died.

Then slowly
the well became
a source of depth
and strength.

She learned
to drink of
the water of life.

Christ had
become
her sufficiency.

Shepherd's Heart

The aroma of wood smoke
lifts me homeward
to the place where I was born,
then
to a grazing field
where shepherds
warmed in the cold night
and angels painted
with the colors of heaven.
All heaven spoke
to our restless, eternal hearts,
and called us to be one
with our creator
and the pride of
His Shepherd's heart.

Still, Deep River

My soul
is bleached
by the desert heat
of living.
I hunger
for the green pastures
in the cool shade
of my Shepherd's voice.

I thirst
for drink
from the still, deep
River of God.

My roots
are gnarled
and my leaves
limp pale.

I must go to the River.

Though the desert calls me,
the River knows my name.

Sweet Chariots are Coming

I listen with head tilted and ear cupped.
I hear them coming in the east
as subtly as the rising of the sun.

I hear them with my soul now
as they reach a crescendo at noon.
The music pounds in my chest
and I join them in glad song.

I rest now.
The music has softened
as the sun sets in the west.
I lay me down to sleep
in the cradle of the night.

I awaken daily
as they ride
again and again
from the east.

One day the chariot will stop
and I will be a part of its song.

Swing low, sweet chariot,
coming for to carry me home...
no more sinking in the west.
I am home.

One-Breath Poems IV

In a Whisper

The greatest truth is whispered.
"I love you."
God said it
through his Son.

Joy's Song

Birds wake the day with their morning song of joy.
Their music becomes mine as the day opens my heart to His joy.

Meekness

Bending low, I met God...
tall, caring, tender and real.
"Blessed are the meek, for they shall inherit the earth." Matthew 5: 5

Hope is

knowing that someone cares...
even when we have ceased to care for ourselves.
"Cast all you anxiety on Him, because He cares for you." I Peter: 7

Humility Is God's way of defining servanthood.

The Pauper's Prayer

You had a lifetime
of pain...
daily.
Your loneliness
filled
an empty,
borrowed room.
Your possessions
could be held on
loose finger tips.
Your fear
ate away constantly
from your mind.
What was left
was a body
too weak
to fight any longer
or even to speak.
You could hear
death whispering
your name.
You surrendered
without remorse.
Free of pain,
death lifted you
as a little child

to take you home
at the end of a full day.

If we will listen closely
we can hear him speak
in death's ear,
"Thank you, my friend."

Share the Warm

I am the man,
the woman,
the mother
and child
that you could not see
when you prayed
in your warm home
for those who were
COLD
and on the streets.

I was first of all *scared*
and then I was *cold*.

I was very alone and sick,
crouched against a wall
praying with all the hope
I had left
that there would be
food tomorrow
and a warm blanket
to hold the next night.

I am the one
you prayed for last night.

The Song of True Rest

I have slept
to the song
of the whippoorwill,
the owl
and the frog.

In my heart
I know
that true rest
is to the song
of a hammer
and nail
in the flesh
of one
who sings
the song of
forgiveness
and
eternal love.

I call Him
Savior,
Lord,
and Friend

Thirst No More

Ease my panting heart,
Lord.

I have run from task
to task
until,
like a fire,
they have dried the cells of my spirit.

I thirst for a still island
surrounded by you—

The River of Life.

"I will extend peace to her like a river,
and the wealth of nations like a flooding stream."
Isaiah 66: 12 (NIV)

Tomorrow I'll Create a Man

When God decided to create a universe,
he took very small shiny marbles
from the vest pocket of his shirt.

He hurled them out with a laugh.
Then, with the snap of his thumb,
froze them in perfect orbit
and commanded them to shine
until he called them home.

He then took one last marble …
his favorite…
he kissed it and moistened it
with his tears.

He dropped it down…down…
and then had it stop and float
in perfect composition
he thought…an original,
his one masterpiece.
He started to leave, but stopped.
He smiled, as though he had
a pleasant thought.
With a laugh like thunder,
he spoke,
"Tomorrow I will create
a man."

What is Going to Be

Waves, like bowling balls,
roll down the beach
until they get small as marbles bursting
and going everywhere.

God pulls them together again
as they wash the white sand
where castles stood and children played.

Like leaning towers of Pisa
they surrender to the hand of God
who put them there.

Like toys He plays with
for me to see.

So I'll know He is power,
and set my sails
to the movement
of creation's breath
that brings me rushing
back home to Him.

Like laughter
I return to His smile,
and the throne

He fashioned for me
on His knees,
in the eternal sand of creation,
told on papyrus rolls
dry and crumbling into the dusk,
that erases all that was...

and I hear the story God tells
of what is going to be.

Where You Are

Wherever you are,
God,
I am.

Where you are
there is my confidence,
my strength and joy.

I am lifted
with every breath
I breathe,
for you are in it
and me.

You Are Mine

The burdens and pressures
are not yours to bear.
They are mine.

The fears that intimidate
I want to lift.
They are mine.

I work from above.
My wisdom is complete.
You are mine.

Live and love relaxed
in the *Joyful Spirit*.
You are mine.

You are mine.
Encourage others
with the strength I give.

You are mine.

*"Come to me, all you who are weary and burdened,
and I will give you rest.*

Grafton Pressley

Take my yoke upon you and learn from me,
for I am gentle and humble in heart,
and you will find rest for your souls.
For my yoke is easy and my burden is light."
Matthew 11: 28 – 30 (NIV)

Young as Thirty Three

He was here only
thirty three years
and no one
fully
recognized Him.

When some
thought they did
they killed him
on a cross.

Our tears
will trail us
through eternity
when we know
what we have done
to God.

But He will
turn our tears
into joy.

That is why
He came
and let himself
be known
and loved.

Your Creator

I see your thoughts
before you think
or speak them.

I am your God.

I imaged you
before you became a cell,
a wish or a prayer.

I know where I lead you.

It is where you want to be.

It is more than you can imagine
or believe.

It is my gift to you
for eternity.

I am your God,
your Creator,
infinite Lord
and personal Friend.

About the Author

Grafton Presley is a United Methodist Pastor in North Georgia. A native of Norcross, Georgia, he holds degrees from Greenville College in Greenville, Illinois and Asbury Theological Seminary in Wilmore, Kentucky.

He and his wife Carol attend the Decatur First United Methodist church in Decatur, Georgia, where he serves as an associate pastor.

Printed in the United States
40723LVS00004B/1-153